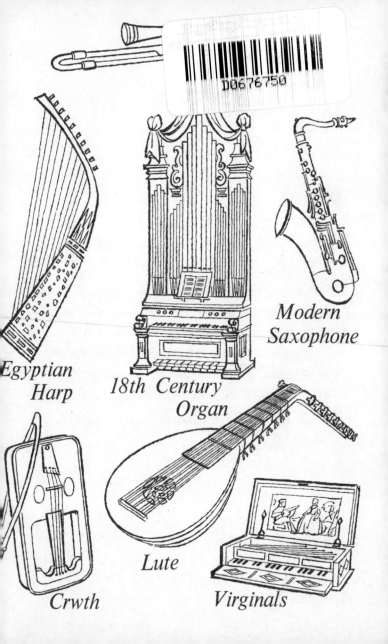

Egyptian
Harp

18th Century
Organ

Modern
Saxophone

Crwth

Lute

Virginals

A Ladybird Book
Series 662

Here is a Ladybird book for children — and adults — who want to know 'how, when, where and why?'

It tells the story of music from the days of Stone Age man up to the present day. It will enhance everyone's appreciation of music, and remind us — in these days of transistors — that there is a great deal of music that should be really listened to with all our attention.

The 24 full-colour illustrations are superb!

2/6
NET

THE STORY OF
MUSIC

by GEOFFREY BRACE

with illustrations by
MARTIN AITCHISON

Publishers : Wills & Hepworth Ltd Loughborough

First published 1968 © *Printed in England*

Music in the Stone Age

The first example we have of man making music is in a prehistoric cave painting in Ariège, in France. It shows a hunter covered with an animal skin, chasing a reindeer. He has a bow, but he is not using it to shoot at the reindeer. He is holding it to his open mouth and playing it like a Jew's Harp—twanging the string and changing the note by altering the shape of his mouth.

Why is he doing this instead of shooting? The answer to this question tells us one of the most important things about the first music. The hunter is, in fact, trying to *cast a spell* on the reindeer.

To the first men, music seemed like magic, and magic was the main reason behind any music-making. The simple shouts, claps, chest-beating and foot-stamping of early tribes had the power, so they believed, to bring rain, cure sickness and make crops grow.

It is easy to understand why even the simplest music-making was thought to have magic powers. It was, after all, something man had created *himself*, from his own mind. It must have seemed like a gift from the gods, and early man probably thought that it gave him some of the power of the gods to help him tame wild animals.

4

The music of the cave men.

The First Musical Instruments

Later huntsmen began to devise other ways of making music. They made rattles of pods and dried seeds, drums of stretched skin on hollow logs, cymbals and gongs from beaten metal, xylophones from rows of different-sized stones.

They made harps from bows (like our hunter's bow) with several strings of different lengths. They put hollow boxes on them to act as resonators, thereby making possible the later invention of the guitar and violin.

They made pipes from hollow bones or bamboo and blew across the top of them as you might across a milk bottle. They tied several different sizes together for different notes. Later they discovered how holes in the side would change the notes. They put thin cane or reed in the top of a bamboo or bone, and made the sound shriller (as when you blow on a leaf held tightly between your thumbs), or inserted a block of wood to make a whistle effect.

They blew down animals' horns and later made metal versions of these horns, straightened out to become trumpets.

By the time of the great empires of Egypt and China, there were many variations of these main types of musical instrument. In the great palaces and temples there were often assemblies of harp, drum, trumpet and pipe players for the worship of the gods and of the King himself.

Musicians in Ancient Egypt playing a harp, double reedpipe and a lute.

Music in the Old Testament

The Old Testament tells us a lot about the part music played in the lives of the early peoples, its association with magic, the worship of various gods and the worship of the Hebrew God, Jehovah.

The destruction of the walls of Jericho by the blowing of trumpets is a story of music making things happen miraculously. So, in a way, is the soothing of Saul's anger by David's harp. Another interesting story is the one about David dancing before the Ark. Dancing was considered just as suitable as singing and playing for worshipping a god, and still is in some countries.

There are many accounts of big celebrations and services being accompanied by music and dancing, and the Bible includes, of course, the Psalms of David, still sung at Jewish and Christian services. The music for singing the psalms has changed over the centuries, although if you go to a Jewish synagogue, you will hear tunes that cannot be very different from the earliest ones.

Many instruments are mentioned in the Bible. Some have strange names, but they are all related to the types we mentioned on Page 6. Shawms, for instance, were reed pipes, psalteries were harps and tabors were drums.

A trumpet, called a 'shofar' is still blown at the Jewish New Year festival.

A harp, lyre, pipe and silver trumpet being played in Solomon's temple.

Music in Greece and Rome

Although the Greeks left us beautiful buildings, fine statues, great poems and plays, their music does not seem to have had the same lasting value.

However, they attached great importance to music and even held contests in singing and playing at the Olympic games. They invented the method of calling notes by letters, and even wrote these letters above the words of songs so that we have a rough idea what the tunes were. The manner of performance would not be as good as that of a trained singer of today, and might sound rather tuneless to our ears.

The main Greek instruments were the 'kithara' and the 'aulos'. The 'kithara' (often called a lyre) was used for accompanying hymns to the gods; the 'aulos' (a double reedpipe) for dancing. Music played an important role in Greek plays, which often used a 'chorus' (the word is Greek) to sing parts of a play.

Greek plays were originally a form of worship to the gods, and music was included for its magical and religious connections. The Romans used music more in their entertainments than in religious ceremonies. It was probably in Rome that the idea of 'strolling players' originated. Poor people who could dance, tumble, juggle, act, play and sing would entertain at the arena and in great houses, and travel all over the Roman Empire, entertaining the ordinary people. These were the first wandering minstrels.

Greek musicians playing a double reedpipe, a hand drum, a lyre and a sambake.

Music of the Early Church

The first Christians were Jews. When they met together for worship they wanted to sing, so they sang what they already knew—the Psalms; and they probably sang them to the old Jewish tunes.

As Christianity spread, each country used its own familiar tunes for the psalms and hymns, so that the music differed widely from place to place.

When the Church became a highly organised institution, it was decided to lay down some definite rules about church music. Under the direction of Pope Gregory the Great, a book was compiled of the proper tunes to be sung for each psalm, hymn and Bible reading, and teachers were sent all over Europe to train choirs and make sure the proper tunes were used. Gregorian chant, as this collection of music is called, is still to this day the basis of music used in the services of the Roman Catholic Church. The origin of the tunes is still a mystery, but they probably grew out of the old Jewish psalm tunes and other popular melodies from the Middle East.

Due to the wandering minstrels, instruments had become very much associated with dancing and merry-making and were thought unsuitable for church. Only the organ was used, which was at this time a very primitive affair with only a few pipes and huge keys that had to be struck with fists or hammers.

An early church choir receives instruction.

Writing Music

Pope Gregory could not have standardized church music without some system of music writing to make sure people sang the right tune each time, and that they did not forget or alter it too much between performances.

There was in fact a simple system of music writing in use at this time. Little marks called '*neumes*' were placed above the words to remind the singer (who would know the tune already) approximately how the notes went up or down. This was how Gregorian Chant was established. You can see why it was necessary to send somebody out to tell the choirs *exactly* what to do.

Later, music copyists spaced out the signs to give a clearer idea of rise and fall. They also ruled a line above the words, making that line a certain note and putting the neumes on, or near, or far away from it as the tune moved around that note. Later still, they ruled two lines, then four, to make the spacing of the notes more exact.

For many years, music was written on four lines with an improved system of notes—heavy black squares, diamonds and oblongs. This is still used for Gregorian Chant and can be seen in some hymn books. It is called 'plainsong notation'.

Music writing using 'neumes'.

The First Composers

By about 1250, the method of writing music in 'neumes' had developed into a reasonably accurate system. The notes were written on ruled lines (at first four in number—sometimes coloured), with different signs for long (¶) and short (♦) notes. This system was known as 'interval notation' and was the beginning of the present day system of music writing.

It was now possible for the musician to sit down before a blank sheet of paper, and *compose* a piece of music. Church musicians were quick to use the advantages that this system gave them to introduce much more elaborate music, because of the exactness of the instructions that could now be given to the singers.

Instead of the whole choir singing the same tune and words, it could be split into groups, and whilst one group might be singing the main tune, other groups, or soloists, could sing variations, more quickly and in higher or lower notes, weaving in and out of the main tune. Because they had been worked out beforehand by the composer, all the different parts blended together harmoniously. This was called 'harmonising', or 'part singing', and required highly skilled and trained singers.

The Church approved of no instruments except the organ, but a few notes might be struck on a harp and vielle at the start of each verse. Organs were sometimes quite big, but rather crude, and the preference for purely vocal music was best shown by the words of the Abbot of Rievaulx in Yorkshire, who wrote . . . 'Why, I pray you, this terrible blowing which evokes the noise of thunder rather than the sweetness of the human voice!"

Ruled lines and special signs help a musician to compose some music.

Minstrels and Troubadours
in the Middle Ages

Wandering singers, recounting the great legends of the past, had existed since the famous Greek story-teller—Homer. A minstrel led the Normans on to the beach at Hastings. Every prince and king in Europe in the Middle Ages had his minstrel to sing to him and his guests at supper. He would sing the story of some great hero: Beowulf, Siegfried, King Arthur or Roland, etc. The songs were very long, sometimes over a thousand lines, and the tune was only a short snatch repeated the same for every line. The story was the main thing!

Minstrels accompanied themselves with a few notes on some simple stringed instrument. They seem to have been the first to bring bowed instruments to Europe from the East—the 'crwth' (crooth), flat and oblong, (see the end-papers), the 'rebec', small and narrow with three strings, and the 'vielle' or 'fiddle'—like a fat violin and played under the chin like the modern instrument.

About the year 1100, it became fashionable amongst the nobility of Southern France to make up their own songs and get a minstrel to play the music for them. These aristocratic amateurs were called 'troubadours' and their northern counterparts 'trouvères', and should not be confused with the humbler (though more expert) minstrel. Richard I was a 'trouvère' and Blondin was his minstrel.

Minstrels arrive to entertain the king and his guests.

The King's Music and Church Music during the Middle Ages

The royal courts and ducal palaces of Italy, France, Flanders and England were the centres of artistic and musical activity in Europe during the fourteenth and fifteenth centuries.

Many of the kings and princes (like our own Henry V) were good musicians, and employed composers to write music for them to sing and play with their friends at court—usually songs in three or four parts, mostly for men's voices and perhaps accompanied by vielle, recorder or lute.

There were also stately dances to tunes played on various instruments, and sometimes elaborate processions and charades with music, scenery and costume which were the beginnings of ballet.

But the greatest musical achievement of this age was the magnificent church music written by the choirmasters of the royal chapels—men like John Dunstable in England, Guillaume Dufay and Josquin des Prés in France, the first 'great' composers.

By this time, the rather haphazard putting together of tunes had developed into a skilled craft of composition for the four types of voice which we now call soprano, alto, tenor, bass. These composers wrote anthems (called 'motets') and completely new settings of the Catholic Mass, in which the different voices keep up a constant ebb and flow of separate melodies, yet blending in rich harmony. This is still some of the finest church music ever written.

A Court procession in the Middle Ages.

The Music of the People

What of the ordinary people of the towns and villages? They rarely had the opportunity to hear the fine music of the cathedrals. Their church music was the plain 'official' chants, and their 'entertainment' music still the stories, songs, dances and tumbling of the minstrels.

But on a great feast day, or fair day, everyone took a holiday and there were plenty of opportunities for merrymaking—and music. There might be the 'waits' (the town band) to open the day with a fanfare of cornetts (wooden trumpets), shawms (harsh reed instruments), sackbuts (old trombones) and pommers (bassoons). There might also be a 'mystery play' performed on carts in the square, telling some Bible story. This would have songs in it (the famous Coventry Carol comes from a 'mystery play').

Plough Monday (the first Monday of the year) brought out the Sword dancers and Mumming Players. May Day saw the strange procession of Hobby Horse, Fool, Green Man and Man-Woman accompanied by a team of Morris Dancers with pipe and tabor—all dating back into remotest times of pagan worship but now just a good excuse for a show and a romp.

Everyone joined in simple circle and line dances, probably to the sound of the bagpipes—a favourite dancing instrument not only in Scotland but in every country in Europe.

Merrymaking and music on a feast day.

Music in Elizabethan Times

In 1501 the first printed music was published by an Italian called Petrucci. Other printers and publishers quickly followed in all the great European capitals, so that it became possible for people outside the monasteries and courts to perform the music of the professional composers employed there.

Music became a very fashionable recreation for the wealthy businessmen and merchants of Elizabethan England. Many great houses had their resident composers, and possessed sets of music and instruments which their owners played and sang. The gentlemen and ladies would gather round with their music and sing quite elaborate and difficult songs (called 'madrigals'). They would also take their instruments and play dances (like the Pavan and Galliard), and instrumental music (Fantazias and Variations on popular songs).

The usual instruments were:

Viols—bowed instruments in various sizes, always played on the knee or floor, never under the chin.

Lute—a large pear-shaped instrument like a big mandolin; as popular then as the guitar is now and used similarly to accompany songs, simply or intricately, and to play solos.

Virginals—a little keyboard instrument like a piano in a box, which could be played on a table. It had a very quiet, tinkling tone.

Among the leading composers of Elizabethan England were William Byrd, Thomas Morley and John Dowland.

Music in a wealthy Elizabethan home.

Protestant Music

The Protestants, who broke away from the Roman Catholic Church in the sixteenth century, were very anxious that everyone should be able to join in the singing in church. Religious songs were therefore written in the language of the country, not in Latin, and with tunes that were easy enough for all to sing and harmonised in a simple fashion so that the tune could be clearly heard.

We still use many of these sixteenth century tunes. The names of the Englishmen, Tallis and Gibbons, and of French and German composers, can be found many times in any Church of England hymn book.

The organ was important in leading the congregational singing. It had long been available, though usually with very few notes and pipes. Now it had many more notes and was used for solo pieces before and after services.

In the seventeenth and eighteenth centuries, bands of instrumentalists were used much more in both Protestant and Catholic churches. On special days, quite long, complicated pieces for soloists, a large chorus and orchestra were performed. They were called 'cantatas' or (if very long) 'oratorios'. Among the finest of these are 'Vespers and Magnificat' by Monteverdi and 'The Passion according to St. Matthew' by Bach.

Protestant Church music in the eighteenth century.

The First Operas in the Seventeenth Century

Acting out a simple story in music, dance and song was a favourite pastime in the courts of France and England from the sixteenth century. Such performances were called 'masques' or 'ballets'.

In the seventeenth century, the splendour-loving rulers of Europe, like Louis XIV of France, produced very spectacular entertainments in which they often took part themselves. These were plays based on tales of Ancient Greece, with fantastic scenery and costume, and with songs, dances and instrumental items specially composed by a professional musician (Louis XIV employed the composer Lulli). The music was played by a highly trained orchestra using that wonderful new Italian instrument called the 'violin'. Everything was set to music—even the ordinary conversation of the play was sung to a sort of singing speech called 'recitative'— a new Italian idea.

These were the first operas. They also mark the appearance of the beginnings of the orchestra, for it was in these operas that violins, flutes, oboes and bassoons were first heard. The orchestral introductions (called 'overtures') to these operas were the forerunners of the purely orchestral music which we hear in concerts today.

The first public opera house was opened in Venice in 1637 and opera was the principal entertainment of the aristocracy for about a hundred years.

Opera at the Court of Versailles.

The First Concerts

The idea of the general public paying to hear other people play and sing, spread from opera to other music. Many writers were producing music for the violin, flute and oboe with accompaniment on the harpsichord— the usual accompanying instrument of the time—which had a keyboard similar to a piano, but in which the strings were plucked—not struck—when the keys were pressed. This music was written mainly for the pleasure of the players themselves, not for an audience. However, the same thing happened in music as in football and cricket later on! What started as a private pastime became a public entertainment!

The first public concerts were given by an English violinist, John Banister, who opened up his house for that purpose when he had been dismissed from the service of King Charles II. He held a concert every Thursday and charged one shilling. The music probably consisted of songs, duets and trios for violins, flutes, etc., with only a few performers.

Public concerts by larger orchestras and choirs were first given in Paris by A. D. Philidor—as a substitute for opera on holy days, when the opera house was closed. They were called 'Concerts Spirituels', but were not entirely religious.

In Germany, after 1673, there were musical evenings given in St. Mary's Church, Lübeck, by the organist Dietrich Buxtehude. Bach once walked 200 miles to attend one of these.

Impression of Banister's room, with flute, harpsichord, 'cello and violin.

Ballads and Broadsides

There was still a large part of the population which did not have the money, or the inclination, to go to the opera house or the concert hall. Their music was still the songs and dances of their own villages, handed down traditionally, plus any new songs picked up from the wandering ballad sellers.

These were the descendants of the old minstrels. They sang in the streets of towns and villages, selling copies of their songs on long printed sheets called 'broadsides'. There was not often any music on the sheet; that had to be remembered from the ballad-seller, or an already-known tune was sung.

Ballads were sometimes historical, and celebrated some great event like the Jacobite rebellion or the Battle of Trafalgar. More often they told of local murders, suicides, disasters, criminals or political characters. Ballad sellers continued to operate in England right up to about a hundred years ago, and some old people still remember broadsides their parents sang. Songs like 'Admiral Benbow' and 'Turpin Hero' have become part of our traditional, national music. Equivalents of the English ballad sellers existed in France, Germany, the Low Countries and America, where their songs may still be heard under the heading of 'folksongs'.

Ballad sellers of the eighteenth century.

The Beggar's Opera—
the First 'Musical Show'

We have seen that up to the eighteenth century there was opera for the aristocracy and broadsides for the poor, but there was not much musical entertainment for the middle classes.

This gap was filled, in England at any rate, by the production in 1723 of 'The Beggar's Opera'. This is an important landmark in musical history—the first popular musical entertainment staged in a public theatre. In fact it was the first 'musical show'—a play, interspersed with songs of popular appeal, in this instance with well-known, popular tunes of the day (such as 'Golden Slumbers' and 'Lili Burlero'), with new words to fit the story. The play, about low London life, highwaymen and criminals, was written by John Gay; the music arranged by a German, Dr. Pepusch.

This new mixture of spoken dialogue and simple songs and choruses became known as 'ballad opera', and paved the way for the comic operas of Offenbach and Gilbert and Sullivan in the nineteenth century.

Another new musical activity emerged at about this period. This was the writing of new popular songs (neither broadsides nor folksongs) by professional composers for unskilled amateurs who liked to sing or play a pleasant tune. So were born such well-known airs as 'Sally in our Alley' by Henry Carey and 'Cherry Ripe' by James Hooke, and the host of later songs that our Victorian great-grandparents sang round the piano.

A scene from 'The Beggar's Opera'.

The Growth of the Large Orchestra

By the beginning of the nineteenth century, concert-going had become a popular, middle-class activity. Concert halls were built and permanent orchestras were established—symphony orchestras as we know them with strings, wind, brass and percussion.

Composers concentrated on writing music for these orchestras—symphonies (long orchestral compositions in several sections), concertos (similar pieces with a soloist) and descriptive pieces (telling stories or describing scenes).

The first notable symphonies were those of Haydn and Mozart. Beethoven is usually considered the greatest writer in this style and he was followed by Schubert (who also wrote many lovely songs), Brahms, Tchaikowsky, Sibelius, and many other composers up to the present time. Descriptive pieces, setting scenes, moods or stories to music, were written by Berlioz (Roman Carnival), Mendelssohn (Fingal's Cave), Debussy (The Sea) and many others. Orchestral music of the nineteenth century is still the favourite kind of listening for many music-lovers.

The modern orchestra can be made to produce a wide variety of sounds, and some present-day composers experiment widely with these so-called 'tone colours'. A few no longer write for instruments at all, but compose from sounds that can be produced on recording tape and by electric currents.

36   *A symphony orchestra.*

The Piano

One of the most important musical instruments of the last hundred years has been the piano. Before the days of records and radio, many people had to rely on arrangements for the piano of symphonies and overtures in order to hear them at all, and since its invention, countless people have been introduced to music.

The piano was developed from earlier keyboard instruments such as the virginals and harpsichord, and the first specimens were built by an Italian called Cristofori in 1709. They were not popular at first—people still preferred the harpsichord, which blended better with stringed instruments.

However, about the year 1800, musical fashions tended towards more dramatic music with big contrasts of volume, and then the piano became more popular. Its biggest advantage over the harpsichord was that it could play softly or loudly (in Italian words—'piano' or 'forte'—hence the name). The pianist can control the volume of every note but this is not possible with the harpsichord.

Nineteenth-century pianos were much stronger than the first ones had been, with heavy iron frames and other improvements which made it possible to produce an enormous and impressive sound.

Piano recitals in private houses and in public halls were a very popular part of musical life in Victorian times. Many of the great pianists of that period had an enormous following. Composers such as Beethoven, Schumann, Chopin and Liszt were themselves excellent pianists, and some of their finest music was written for the piano. With so much wonderful music available, it is not surprising that the piano recital has, for a long time, been a very popular part of musical life.

Liszt playing Beethoven's 'Moonlight Sonata' to friends.

The Development of Opera

The earliest operas were mainly for the aristocracy and had little appeal to ordinary people. Even so, many great opera houses were built in the big European cities. In Germany and Italy every fair-sized town had, and still has, its own opera house and company. The earliest operas are not often performed nowadays. Most of those produced today have been written in the last one hundred and fifty years or so.

It was Mozart who first made opera into something more than just a dressed-up performance of beautiful music. An opera like his 'Marriage of Figaro', for instance, has a good story, plenty of action and some very funny scenes. It is all music, with no speech, and on a grander scale than a musical show, but full of easily-remembered tunes.

In England, opera has sometimes been thought a bit 'snobbish', mainly because, for many years, we had only one opera house (at Covent Garden) where seats were rather expensive. The Sadler's Wells Opera Company helped to change that, presenting opera at cheaper prices for the enjoyment of many more people.

Among the many popular operas which give a first-class evening's entertainment to anyone are: Rossini's 'The Barber of Seville', Bizet's 'Carmen' and Smetana's 'The Bartered Bride'. Other well-known opera writers include Puccini, Verdi, Wagner and—in our own time —Benjamin Britten.

A scene from Rossini's opera: 'The Barber of Seville'.

Ballet

Ballet is a display of dancing, usually based on a simple story and accompanied by full-scale orchestral music. Like opera, ballet was first produced for the benefit of the nobility. In fact, opera and ballet were usually combined in one spectacle.

The idea of a whole evening of ballet alone did not become general until the early nineteenth century. Among the first 'pure' ballets were 'Giselle', 'Sylvia'and 'Coppélia', all produced in Paris. It was in these that the traditional female costume of short white frill, or 'tutu', and of men's white tights, first appeared. The French dancers also introduced dancing on 'points' (toe-blocked ballet shoes) and the various set 'postures' or 'positions' of the dancers.

In the late nineteenth century, the Russians took the lead in ballet and have remained prominent ever since. They gave us 'The Nutcracker Suite', 'The Sleeping Beauty' and 'Swan Lake', all to Tchaikovsky's music and, at the beginning of this century 'The Firebird', 'Petrushka' and 'The Rite of Spring' with music by Stravinsky.

America has produced fine modern ballets—'Billy the Kid', 'Rodeo' (music by Copland) and the exciting dancing of Bernstein's 'West Side Story'.

Modern ballet does not use the standard white costumes but whatever costume is appropriate to the story.

A scene from 'The Firebird' ballet.

Musical Shows

The musical show, a spoken play interspersed with songs and dances in popular style, is as successful today as it ever was. Even the older shows are continually revived and enjoyed, especially among amateurs.

Originally called 'ballad opera' because the tunes were well-known ballads of the day (see page 34), this type of entertainment has gone under many different names during the last hundred years, but has always kept to the basic pattern of speech, popular song and dance. Here are some of the later names used, the composers who wrote in this style, and some of their best-known work.

Opéra-bouffe (France): Offenbach—'Orpheus in the Underworld'.

Comic Opera (England): Gilbert & Sullivan—'The Mikado'.

Operetta (Austria): Léhar—'The Merry Widow'.

Musical Comedy (England & America): Romberg—'The Student Prince'.

Musical (America): Rodgers & Hammerstein—'Oklahoma', 'The Sound of Music'.

These are only a few of the highly successful shows written over the last century, which have given us some of our best and most lasting popular songs.

We have mentioned the dancing in 'West Side Story'. Another important feature of this musical is the fact that the story does not end happily. Perhaps this is a clue to how the musical show of the future will develop.

44

A scene from Gilbert & Sullivan's comic opera — 'The Mikado'.

Jazz

What is jazz? We all recognise jazz when we hear it, but have difficulty in saying *exactly* how it differs from other music.

There are two main elements in jazz which give it the distinctive character that makes it so different from anything that went before. One is the playing of instruments so that they sound like the half-shouted, half-sung blues of Negro folksong. The other is the steady, unchanging 1-2-3-4 beat, imitated from the French military marching music the Negroes heard in New Orleans, where jazz was born around 1900.

Another most important feature of jazz is 'improvisation' or 'making it up as you go along'. The skill and speed with which a player does this, and plays some completely new variation of the basic tune, is one of the great thrills of a jazz performance.

Tunes are not the most important feature of jazz. It is not the composer but the performer who makes a good piece of jazz, and it is impossible to write down much of a jazz performance in musical notes.

Jazz has influenced many kinds of music, but particularly popular song—which still borrows from jazz its beat, its singing style and its improvisation.

A jazz player 'improvises' on a basic tune.

Folk or Traditional Songs

One fine summer's morning, in 1903, a certain Mr. Cecil Sharp was strolling in the garden of his friend, the vicar of Hambridge in Somerset. He heard a gardener singing a song, one of the loveliest tunes he had ever heard. The gardener did not know where it came from; he had simply learned it as a boy from other people.

The song was a 'folk' or 'traditional' song called 'The Seeds of Love', passed on from one person to another, but never actually written down.

Sharp realized that it should be possible to find other old songs surviving in the memories of ordinary people. He travelled the country on his bicycle and unearthed several hundred songs which we all now know as English folksongs.

Such songs are still being found—even in big industrial towns and ports like Newcastle and Liverpool, old music-hall and public house songs that most people had forgotten.

They will never die now, for they have been recorded and printed. They have had a new lease of life too from young amateur musicians, who have discovered afresh the beauty of these songs which often have such fine words and rousing choruses.

Cecil Sharp hears a gardener singing a traditional song.

Music All Day!

Not so many years ago, people could hear only a very limited amount of music and few people ever heard it performed by experts.

Today, by means of the radio or a record player, we can hear any music we choose from any period, in any style, played by the finest musicians in the world. What is more, with a record we can hear it as often as we like, and this has completely changed the part music has taken in our daily lives.

Perhaps we have too much music now—and because it is so easily obtained, we make too little effort to listen to it. An enormous amount of music on radio and records is often regarded as just a background to talking, eating or housework. This may make us forget that there is a great deal of music that is meant to be really listened to with all our attention.

However good recorded music might be, it can never really take the place of a live performance. To be present at an actual performance is half the enjoyment of music. Take every opportunity you can to attend concerts and musical gatherings of every kind. Better still, learn to play something and join in the music-making yourself.

Good music unappreciated!

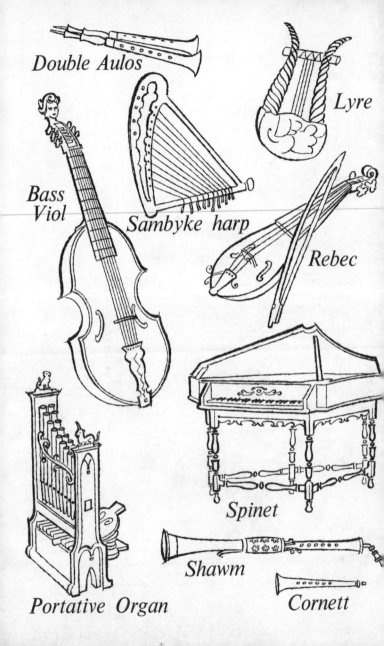

Double Aulos

Lyre

Sambyke harp

Bass Viol

Rebec

Portative Organ

Spinet

Shawm

Cornett